I-DIDN'T-DO-IT-! NOBODY-SAW-ME-! YOU-CAN'T-PROVE-A-THING-!
Attending Prayer Club that day was like wearing a big "guilty" sign !
But...
...start attending regularly, then maybe you don't look quite so guilty.
You're blackmailing me !
Black femaling you, actually. But you get my point.

12-4-TEENS
7:00 PM
C'MON UP !
Sign my court card and lemme go.
Sure -- **after** the meeting !
I already hate this ! Nothing but a buncha losers --
Huh ? ! ? ! What are **you** doing here ?

What's this?

"The 12 Steps to Recovery."

I made copies for newcomers.

The 12 Steps

Here are the steps we took, which are suggested as a program of recovery:

1. We admitted we were powerless over drugs and alcohol, that our lives had become unmanageable.

2. Came to believe that a Power greater than ourselves could restore us to sanity.

3. Made a decision to turn our will and our lives over to the care of God as we understood Him.

4. Made a searching and fearless moral inventory of ourselves.

5. Admitted to God, to ourselves, and to another human being the exact nature of our wrongs.

6. Were entirely ready to have God remove all these defects of character.

7. Humbly asked Him to remove our shortcomings.

8. Made a list of all persons we had harmed, and became willing to make amends to them all.

9. Made direct amends to such people wherever possible, except when to do so would injure them or others.

10. Continued to take personal inventory and when we were wrong promptly admitted it.

11. Sought through prayer and meditation to improve our conscious contact with God as we understood Him, praying only for knowledge of His will for us and the power to carry that out.

12. Having had a spiritual awakening as the result of these steps, we tried to carry this message to others, and to practice these principles in all our affairs.

-- Based on the AA Big Book

Nano-seconds later...

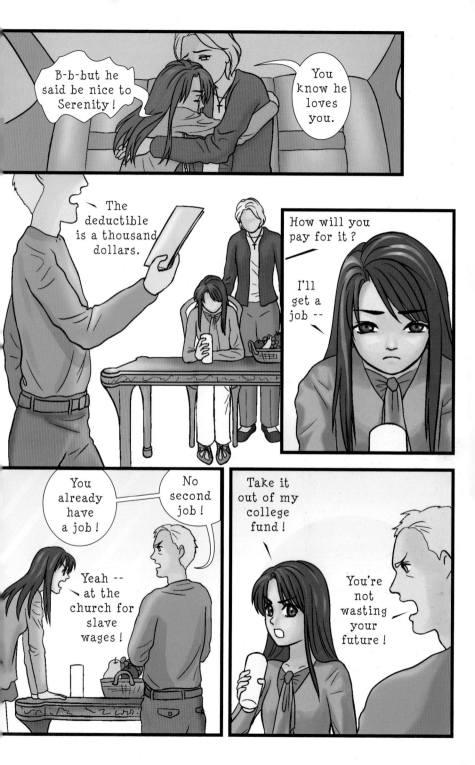

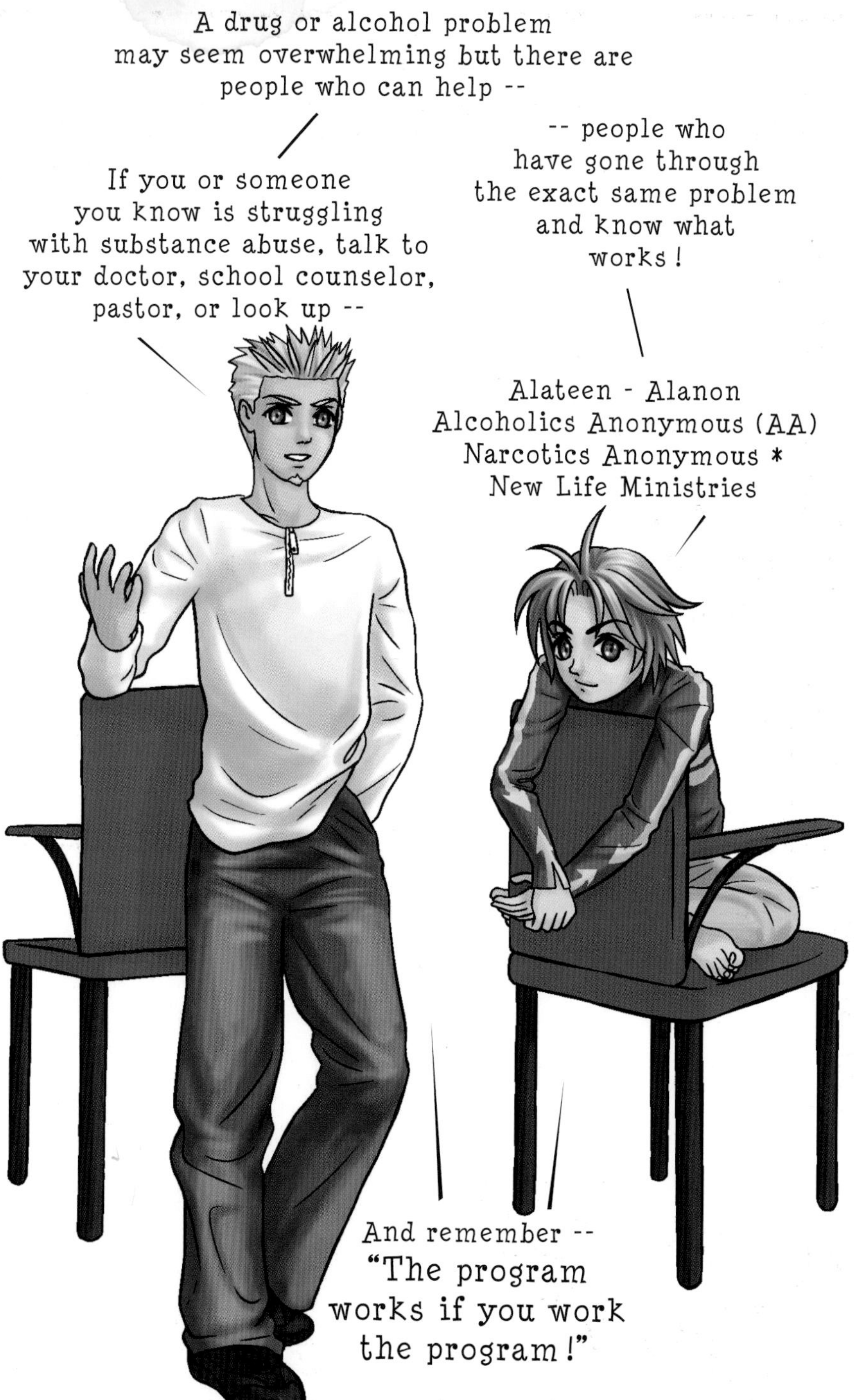

*not to be confused with Narconon

GOOFYFOOT GURL
hitting the beach this September!

THE revolve TOUR

ALL NEW **EVENT** for Teen Girls
PRESENTED BY WOMEN OF FAITH

Hawk Nelson

Natalie Grant

KJ-52

Max & Jenna Lucado

Ayiesha Woods

Chad Eastham

Kimiko Soldati

We're Coming to a City Near You!
TOUR DATES

Columbus, OH
September 14 - 15, 2007

Dallas, TX
September 21 - 22, 2007

Hartford, CT
September 28 - 29, 2007

St. Louis, MO
October 5 - 6, 2007

Anaheim, CA
October 12 - 13, 2007

Sacramento, CA
October 19 - 20, 2007

Philadelphia, PA
November 2 - 3, 2007

Minneapolis, MN
November 9 - 10, 2007

Portland, OR
November 16 - 17, 2007

Atlanta, GA
November 30 - Dec. 1, 2007

Orlando, FL
January 25 - 26, 2008

Charlotte, NC
February 1 - 2, 2008

Denver, CO
February 15 - 16, 2008

Houston, TX
February 22 - 23, 2008

✳ Download **Preview Video** Online

To register by phone, call 877-9-REVOLVE
or online at REVOLVETOUR.COM

Serenity

Created by Realbuzz Studios, Inc.
Min Kwon, Primary Artist

Serenity throws a big wet sloppy one out to:
Stef D. and all of Bill W.'s friends.

Smack!

Luv U Guyz !!!

©&TM 2007 by Realbuzz Studios   ISBN 978-1-59554-384-4

www.Realbuzz Studios.com
www.SerenityBuzz.com

Published by Thomas Nelson, Inc. Nashville, TN 37214 www.thomasnelson.com

Library of Congress Cataloguing-in-Publication Data
Applied For

Scripture quotations marked NCV are taken from
The HOLY BIBLE, New Century VERSION®. NCV®.
Copyright © 2001 by Nelson Bibles.
Used by permission of Thomas Nelson. All rights reserved.

Printed in Singapore.
5 4 3 2 1